13th STREET

The Fire-Breathing Ferret Fiasco

Read more 13th Street books!

HARPER Chapters

The Fire-Breathing Ferret Fiasco

by DAVID BOWLES

illustrated by SHANE CLESTER

HARPER

An Imprint of HarperCollinsPublishers

To my nieces Nikki, Emily, Samantha, and Kaylee, for taking your cousins on such wild adventures. —DB

13th Street #2: The Fire-Breathing Ferret Fiasco
Copyright © 2020 by HarperCollins Publishers
www.harperchapters.com
Library of Congress Control Number: 2019950275
ISBN 978-0-06-294783-3 — ISBN 978-0-06-294782-6 (pbk.)
Typography by Torberg Davern
20 21 22 23 24 PC/LSCC 10 9 8 7 6 5 4 3 2
❖
First Edition

CONTENTS

CHAPTER

BIG SURPRISE AT THE BUS STOP

Dante Dávila hopped down the steps and hit the sidewalk with a smile. He loved his morning stroll to the bus stop!

"Dante!" It was Ms. Cartaya, the mail carrier, slipping letters into mailboxes. "Looking sharp there, cutie."

"Thanks!" Dante said. "First day of school. Got to look my best!"

He gave Ms. Cartaya a thumbs-up and kept walking toward the bus stop.

Just then Mr. Medina came out of his house, coffee in hand. As he bent to pick up his newspaper, he grinned at Dante.

"*¡Buenos días!* Ready to break some hearts, Romeo?"

"Nope!" Dante laughed. "Sharing my good looks with everybody's lucky eyes."

"*¡Eso!*" Mr. Medina said, lifting his cup. "Confidence. The key to life."

A few cars cruised by as Dante neared the corner, their drivers waving hello. *It's nice to be*

back in my own neighborhood, Dante thought. *Everybody loves me here. It's safe. Not like 13th Street.*

As if his thoughts had called her, a woman came stumbling out from behind a tree.

Dante's eyes went wide.

It was Doña Chabela. The strange old lady from Gulf City!

"What are **YOU** doing here?" Dante asked nervously.

"Making sure," she gasped, "you get on that bus. Long ride ahead of you, *guapo*."

CHAPTER

DANGEROUS DETOUR!

With a grinding sound, a school bus came around the corner. It hissed to a stop a few feet away. The door creaked open.

Dante put his foot on the first step, his hand on the metal rail. *If Chabela wants me to get on this bus, maybe I shouldn't*, he thought.

"Hurry up, Dante," said Robby Leal, the young bus driver.

"Be brave!" called Doña Chabela. "Face your fears, boy!"

Dante hurried inside. As the doors shut, his cousin Ivan, who was sitting in their favorite three-seater, pressed his face to the window. He looked shocked.

"No way!" Ivan shouted. "Malia, it's that weird woman from Gulf City!"

Malia was Dante's *other* cousin. She was sitting next to her best friend, Susana Leal, the bus driver's little sister. Susana narrowed her eyes at Dante. They had been rivals since kindergarten, when Dante had been voted Cutest in the Class.

Susana insisted she was **MUCH** cuter then—and even cuter now!

"The ugly duckling's arrived," Susana said under her breath.

Malia ignored her and stood up to see better.

"Doña Chabela? In Nopalitos?" she said.

"Sit down, guys!" Robby told Dante and Malia. They were the only kids onboard this early. The school bus route had barely begun.

"Just drive, Robby," Susana answered.

"You're supposed to respect me, squirt," her brother warned.

"Whatever." Susana checked her face in a small mirror.

"Still not cuter than me," Dante whispered as he took a seat beside Ivan.

Susana shot him an angry look.

Malia sat between them, clearing her throat. "Dante? Did Chabela say anything to you?"

Before Dante could reply, Robby groaned.

A tree lay in the road ahead, just after the next intersection. "Looks like we have to take a quick detour," Robby said.

He spun the steering wheel. The bus began to turn, heading onto the side street.

WHOOSH!

A strange roaring sound swirled around them. The bus shook.

"Wait," said Robby. "I don't recognize this neighborhood."

At the same instant, Ivan, Dante, and Malia jumped up with a gasp!

The bus was surrounded by rusted old cars with no tires. Leaves blew up and down cracked sidewalks. An eternally gray sky hung overhead like a dirty rag.

Below those dense clouds, the tall, crooked, and empty buildings of 13th Street stretched as far as the eye could see.

"Oh no," whispered Dante. "We're . . . back!"

CHAPTER

3

FIRE-BREATHING FERRETS!

Susana closed her mirror. "Back where?"

Robby slowed to a stop. Dante could see the alley where he'd hidden from the Snatch Bats a few months ago.

"Back where we left off," Dante muttered. "Like a video-game checkpoint."

Suddenly six big creatures jumped into the street! They were the size of small horses, but their bodies and tails were longer.

Their fur was thick and slick. They had short snouts and ears.

Susana stared out the window. "Uh, R-Robby? Why are there giant ferrets in the road?"

One of the beasts was in front of the bus. It snarled, showing sharp teeth.

"I don't know, but they don't look friendly!" he replied.

Dante hurried down the aisle to the back door. The creatures were everywhere. "Boss? I think we're in trouble."

Malia took a deep breath. "Robby, you need to drive away. Fast."

The bus driver raised an eyebrow. "That's *Mr. Leal* to you, Malia. And I don't take orders from kids."

"I'd listen to her," Ivan said. "She helped us escape from this place before."

Just then, all the ferrets opened their mouths at once. Dante could see an orange glow at the back of their throats.

Then the creatures **BREATHED FIRE AT THE BUS**!

WHOOSH!

The bus got hot fast. Some of the windows cracked. The kids moved to the aisle, ducking down.

"What kind of ferrets can *breathe fire*?" Robby shouted.

"Giant ones from another dimension!" Ivan replied.

"**JUST DRIVE!**" yelled Malia.

Robby stamped on the gas pedal, and the school bus sped ahead!

VROOOM!

Apartment buildings whizzed by. Now they were in the warehouse district. The ferrets couldn't keep up. Soon Dante couldn't see them anymore.

"We lost the furry flamethrowers," he called, his heart pounding in his chest.

Malia looked at Dante. "Are you okay? You're sweating. **A LOT**."

"He's scared, Malia," Ivan said. "Fire is his big fear."

Susana looked at them, shocked. "What?"

Malia explained. "His seventh birthday. Too much product in his hair. When he went to blow out the candles, **WHOOSH**! Flaming bangs."

"It was terrible," Dante said sadly. "Mom put out the fire, but my hair was ruined. Dad shaved it all off."

Susana managed to smile. "Bald, huh?"

"Don't start, wannabe," Dante warned.

Robby slowed the bus to a stop. "This is crazy. I need answers."

Taking a deep breath, Dante explained. "We spent the summer in Gulf City. A woman told us to take a shortcut. It led us

here, to 13th Street. It's another world. Full of monsters. You have to defeat them to escape."

Robby turned in his seat. "Wait, are you talking about that lady at the bus stop?"

Ivan stood up. "Yes. You know her?"

"Her name is Isabel Aguilar. She lived in Nopalitos when I was in middle school," Robby explained. "She moved away to take care of her grandkids, I think."

Susana adjusted her hair with a shaky hand. "So Mrs. Aguilar sent us here? How? Why?"

Malia shrugged. "Maybe she's an evil witch."

"Yeah," said Dante, "who gets fluffy oversize rodents to roast school buses."

Suddenly there was a **BOOM**. The whole bus shook!

"AHHHH!" screamed everyone.

Except Ivan. "Relax. It's just the metal of the bus shrinking as it cools down."

"Whew," sighed Malia. "I thought we were goners."

Three chapters down! ¡Bien! That means *nice*.

CHAPTER

HIDEY HOLE

Susana sighed. "Well, one mystery is solved."

"What do you mean?" Malia asked.

"When you got to Gulf City, you kept complaining about Thing One and Thing Two. A few weeks later, you guys were best buddies," she explained.

Ivan frowned at Malia. "Thing One and Thing Two?"

"That was before we defeated the Snatch

Bats together," Malia said, embarrassed. "Sorry."

"Y'all can do a group hug later," interrupted Robby. "How do we escape?"

Dante looked back down the street. "In video games, you can run away from the monster for a while. But it keeps coming. We gotta get this bus off the street."

Ivan nodded. "And we need time to make a plan of attack."

Malia pointed. "Look, one of the warehouses is open."

Robby headed toward the building. Its metal door had been rolled up. There was just enough space to drive inside.

The brakes hissed. Everyone exited the bus.

"Let's get that door down, Ivan," Robby said. But they couldn't reach.

"Is there a stool around here?" asked Malia.

"No need," Dante said. "I'll just use my charm!"

Susana rolled her eyes. "You're so conceited."

"And you're jealous. Close up, Kalaan!" Dante shouted the magical command.

The door came slamming down. **WHAM!** Everyone jumped back.

"Good one," Ivan said. "Use that 13th Street magic."

Painted on the inside of the door was a symbol: two lines, one atop the other, with three dots above them.

"What does it mean?" Susana asked. "That question's for Ivan, Dante. Don't strain your cute little head."

"Ha, ha, Miss Runner-up." Dante shrugged. "Lots of doors have that mark. It means they can be opened."

Robby inspected the door. "Suse, go get the chain and padlock from the toolbox."

"I'll go with you," Malia said.

As the two girls headed back to the bus, the sound of thudding steps came from outside, getting louder. Suddenly strange barking and hissing filled the air.

Dante swallowed hard. "They're here!"

CHAPTER

WEASELS REACH THE WAREHOUSE!

"Suse!" Robby shouted.

The two girls were already coming, dragging a chain between them. Susana also held a lock in her hand.

The fire-breathing monsters slammed into the door!

BAM!

Then their claws starting scratching at it!

SKRITCH! SKREECH!

Grabbing the chain from Susana and Malia, Robby bound the door to its frame. As he pulled the chain tight, he motioned to his sister.

"Put the padlock on these links!"

Susana did, and everyone backed away from the door.

Outside, the monsters were chirping and hissing angrily. Some of them got their claws under the door. They tried to lift it. But the chain held.

"That was close," Susana said. "Those ferrets almost got your hair, Dante!"

Dante smirked. "You're hilarious."

"I don't think they're ferrets," Ivan said. "Probably weasels. Big stoats, that's the species."

Dante laughed nervously. "Big? How about gigantic stoats?"

"Weasels, ferrets, whatever," Malia interrupted. "How do we get rid of them? Hiding isn't the answer."

Ivan bit his lip. "We can't get to the Depot of the Dead . . ."

Robby's eyes widened. "The what of the what?"

"Besides, nothing on those shelves would help," Ivan continued.

Dante glanced around. "Hey, this warehouse is full of junk. Maybe we'll find the right tools."

"Good idea," Malia said. "Split up and start searching. We need stuff that can stop fire-breathing ferrets."

Ivan cleared his throat. "Weasels."

"So, what, warmth-breathing weasels? Doesn't quite work," Dante said.

Robby turned his hat around. "Scorching stoats?"

Malia tapped her foot. "Enough jokes. Start looking!"

Everyone hurried to obey her.

Meanwhile, the creatures kept slamming themselves against the door.

CHAPTER

ZIGZAGGING ZOMBIES!

Dante hoped he'd find a fire extinguisher. But no.

The scratching at the door stopped. Then an odd creaking sound began.

URRRRK. CRIIIICK. HURRRM.

Dante stared at the door. In the middle, right below the mysterious symbol, it started glowing.

"Oh no." Dante gulped. "Guys? Guys!"

The others stopped searching and turned around. Except Robby. He was kneeling, looking at something on the floor.

Dante pointed. "The weasels. Are trying. To melt. The door!"

Susana put her hand over her mouth.

Just then, Robby grabbed a ring in the floor and pulled with all his might.

CREAAAK!

A secret trapdoor lifted open!

"There's a ladder going down into a tunnel!" he shouted. "Let's go!"

A piece of white-hot metal fell off the door. Through the hole, Dante could see the hungry face of a giant weasel.

He ran toward Robby and climbed into the tunnel.

Next came Susana, Malia, and Ivan.

The tunnel had a dirt floor. It was barely visible in the light from the open trapdoor.

Robby came down after them. He closed the hatch, leaving them in total darkness.

"Uh, guys?" Dante said, his voice shaky. "I can't see a thing!"

"Hang on," Malia said. "I'll use my phone's flashlight."

She pressed a button and light poured out onto the ground.

"Ew!" Susana said. "Did somebody just fart?"

Malia lifted her phone.

Coming toward them were six people-shaped figures. They stumbled a little as they walked, zigging to one side of the tunnel, then zagging to the other.

"Hello?" Malia said. "We're trying to escape some fire-breathing ferrets. Which way should we go?"

The first two figures got closer. Malia's phone lit up their faces.

It was a man and a woman. But their skin was sort of green. Patches of it were peeling away, too. The man lifted his hand.

Some of his fingers were just bone!

And he smelled like spoiled hamburger meat!

"Oh, great," Ivan muttered. "We're dead."

"No," said Susana, gulping. "*They're* dead!"

WHOA! You outsmarted the ferrets and read six chapters!

CHAPTER

UGH, THE UNDEAD!

"Argh!" growled the man.

"Zombies!" shouted Ivan.

"I got this!" Robby lifted a hammer he'd brought with him.

"Wait!" the man said, raising his other hand. "Just kidding! We're not going to hurt you!"

The woman rolled her eyes. "Please forgive him. He's easily bored."

The other four stepped into the light. They

looked much younger.

"Oh, yay." Susana shuddered. "Zombie kids!"

"Sorry," the man said. "I know we're scary."

The woman nodded. "But come with us. We'll lead you to safety."

Robby was suspicious. "Why should we trust you?"

"We live on this street," the man said. "We know all the hiding places. And we know how important family is. You're a family, right?"

Ivan spoke up. "Two families. Brother and sister. Three cousins."

Malia calmly made introductions. "I'm Malia. That's Ivan and Dante. These two are Robby and Susana."

Dante took a step toward them, trying not to panic. "What are your names?"

"We forgot them." The young girl zombie poked her head between the two adults. "We're just Mictecah now."

"Meek what?" Dante asked.

"Speak English or Spanish to the living," the woman reminded her.

"Sorry. Undead Folk," the girl translated.

"I'm Big Brother," said the tallest of the kids. "She's Sister. This is Little Brother."

The shortest pointed to the other boy zombie. "And he's Cousin."

The woman smiled. "I'm Mother. This is Father."

A horrible screech came from above. Something started pounding against the trapdoor.

"Great!" said Malia. "They know where we are!"

Smoke started curling from the wood above their heads. The fire-breathing ferrets were burning through!

"Follow us!" shouted Mother, shambling away as fast as she could. "There's not much time!"

CHAPTER

8

FREEZE THE FURIOUS FIRE

The zombies ran ahead. The darkness didn't bother them at all. Malia kept shining her light for the living.

Then the ferrets burst into the tunnel behind them! Flames lit up the air like the sun!

"Faster!" Dante shouted. He noticed that Big Brother and Cousin had backpacks on.

Sister and Little Brother were carrying bags with metal parts sticking out of them.

"Do y'all have fire extinguishers?" Dante asked.

Sister looked back at him. "To fight the Cozamah?"

"That means the Furious Fire," Big Brother said, pointing behind them. "And no. We've searched everywhere. No fire extinguishers."

The yowling, hissing, and hot flames of the Furious Fire kept everyone scrambling for cover.

Just as it seemed the wicked weasels would catch them, the group reached another ladder. Climbing up, they entered a huge, gloomy warehouse. There were big shelving units that divided part of the space into separate areas. Dante thought this must be where the zombie family lived.

Father slammed the trapdoor shut. "Big Brother, flood the tunnel!"

Against the wall was a huge pipe with a red valve wheel attached. Big Brother grabbed the wheel and spun it hard. There was a loud groan and then:

WHOOSH!

The sound of rushing water came from beneath their feet.

"You sure this will work?" asked Dante.

"We flood the tunnels all the time," Cousin explained. "Makes it easier to catch the rats."

"Gross! Why are you catching rats?" Dante stared at the zombie boy.

"To eat them, obviously," Cousin replied.

Dante felt sick to his stomach.

"Hey," said Big Brother, laying his leathery hand on Dante's head. "Could be worse. We could eat brains."

The Undead Folk laughed.

"That," Susana announced, "was not funny."

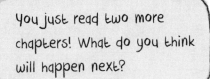

You just read two more chapters! What do you think will happen next?

CHAPTER

9

COLD STORAGE

Dante looked around. "Where's the portal? Didn't we defeat them?"

Mother shook her head. "No, the water just swept them away for now."

Malia sighed. "There's got to be something else we can try. What do we know about weasels?"

"Before Suse was born," Robby said, "when I was a little younger than you all, our family used to travel up north to work in the fields.

I would go to school there a few months each year. Once I had this great teacher, a Native American man. His family had been weasel trappers for generations."

Everyone moved closer, paying careful attention to Robby's story.

"He told us things about the animals. Tribes had different ideas about them, but most agreed that they were bad luck. Dangerous. Except in their ermine stage."

"What's that?" Dante asked.

Ivan jumped in. "Weasels' bodies know when winter comes. They shed their darker fur and turn white. You call them ermine then."

"Right," Robby agreed. "Stories say they are gentler when they're white. They're good luck, too."

"So," Dante said, "when is winter around here?"

Father shook his head. "There's no winter on 13th Street."

Susana was upset. "You're a big help, Robby."

"Susana, we don't need winter," Ivan explained. "We just need to create a cold and dark environment."

Father gestured around him. "That's what this used to be. We woke up here five years ago, when the Quiet Prince arrived. It's not much, but it's the only home we remember."

Dante wondered who the Quiet Prince was, but before he could ask, Robby spoke up. His question would have to wait.

"If this is a refrigerated warehouse, why is it so warm?" he asked.

"The generator stopped working," Big Brother told him, holding up his backpack. "That's why we were in the tunnels. We've been scavenging for fuel and metal parts."

Sister pulled a quart of motor oil from her bag. "We need the cold so we don't rot to pieces."

"Ah, that explains the stink," Dante whispered.

"Dante, not cool." Malia elbowed her cousin.

Ivan took the plastic container from Sister's hand. "Robby? You've fixed generators before, right?"

"Yup," Robby said. "They're just motors, like in the bus. But I'd need help."

"Lucky you," Ivan told him. "Last year I did my science fair project on the combustion engine."

Susana laughed. "You're such a nerd."

Dante shook his head. "I don't get it. How does the generator help us?"

"If me and Ivan can get it working," Robby explained, "this warehouse will cool down quick. Then all we've got to do is lure the Furious Fire inside. They should shift into their white winter coats."

"Brilliant plan, Robby," said Father.

Dante noticed Susana glancing at her big brother. She was trying not to show how  she felt. But her eyes glittered with pride.

Robby nodded at Father. "Thanks. Come on, Ivan. Let's help the Undead Folk."

Malia raised her right index finger. "And tame the fire-breathing ferrets. Don't forget that part."

"I just had a thought," Ivan said. "What if those sneaky stoats melted the bus?"

"Only one way to find out," Malia said.

"While you and Robby get this place cold, the Cutie Twins and I will go check things out. Besides, we need to know where the weird weasels are if we're going to herd them back here."

Dante gulped. "Oh, snap."

CHAPTER

10

RISKY RECON

A few minutes later, Susana, Dante, and Malia climbed to the top of the warehouse. They leaped from rooftop to rooftop, back to the abandoned bus.

"This is a lot easier without Snatch Bats attacking," Dante said.

"They must have been after your award-winning face," Susana teased.

Malia turned and stopped them. "Ugh. I'm

so sick of you two. Dante, Susana is my best friend. She's awesome and smart. Stop being a competitive jerk."

Susana smiled and raised an eyebrow at Dante.

"And you," Malia said, turning to her friend, "knock off your jealous insults. My cousin isn't some empty-headed pretty boy. He's good and brave and clever."

Dante didn't know what to say. There was this strange lump in his throat.

"Thanks, Boss." He looked at Susana. "Sorry. Can we try to be friends, too?"

Susana nodded. "Sure. We can try, Dante."

They shook hands, then walked in silence until they reached the warehouse where they'd left the bus. Malia went down the stairway first, carefully opening  the door and peering inside.

"What do you see, Boss?" Dante asked.

"The coast is clear," Malia said.

The warehouse was a disaster. The door

had been completely melted away. Shelves had been knocked down. Office doors were torn off their hinges.

The bus was fine except for the burn marks from the first attack.

"Whew!" sighed Dante. Then he saw it, out of the corner of his eye.

A fire extinguisher.

"Yes!" he shouted, running to pick it up.

Malia put
a finger to
her lips. She
walked toward
the entrance.
Susana
and Dante
followed.
They poked
their heads

outside. Down the street toward the
zombies' warehouse, there was no sign of
the ferrets.

Then the kids turned to look the other
way and saw them. A group of giant weasels,
curled up together beside a rusted garbage
truck. Some were grooming themselves like
dogs or cats. One stood up and shook itself,
spraying water everywhere.

The kids slipped back inside.

"Good," Malia said. "When Robby starts the bus, they'll come running. Then someone can just herd them to the Undead Folk."

"Easier said than done," Susana replied.

Just then, a noise came from inside one of the warehouse offices.

The kids spun around.

One of the ferrets jumped out, its mouth open and glowing orange!

"Run!" Malia hurried toward the stairs.

Dante was frozen in place. The monster moved toward him.

"Dante!" Susana grabbed Dante's arm.

Then Dante looked down at the fire extinguisher. He pulled the metal pin. Lifted the nozzle. And when the angry weasel got close enough, he pulled the trigger.

WHOOSH!!!

The foam hit the creature's mouth! Its fire went out, and the ferret dropped to the ground, knocked out cold.

Dante sighed in relief.

CHAPTER

11

TIME TRAVEL

A couple hours later, the Undead Folk's warehouse was freezing. Susana, Malia, and Dante were guarding the rooftop while final adjustments were made to the generator.

The air seemed even gloomier when Ivan and Robby joined them, along with the zombie dad.

"Someone has to lead the Furious Fire into our building," Father explained. "I volunteer."

"You sure?" Dante asked.

"It's the least I can do to repay you," the zombie replied.

After they crossed to the next roof, Robby cleared his throat. "I'm worried, little dudes. We've been here a long time. What do I tell your parents? The school?"

"Easily solved," Father said. "Portals can open into the past, just never before the moment you entered this world. Reset your watches and clocks to an earlier hour. Then pass through the portal."

"Oh, wow," said Ivan. "So the flow of time between worlds is impacted by its measurement?"

"Hush, nerd," Malia said. "We're here."

They descended into the wrecked warehouse. The weasel Dante had fought was still unconscious on the floor.

The zombie dad reached out his hand. Robby shook it.

"Thanks, friends," Father said. "We wish you well."

"Stay frosty!" Dante said. Everyone groaned.

"On the bus, guys," Malia ordered. "No time to waste!"

"Well, actually," Ivan said, "now that we know about time-shifting, we could . . ."

"Don't 'well, actually' me, Ivan Eisenberg. We're not staying here a second longer than we have to." Malia gave him a little push toward the open doors of the bus.

Once on board, Malia and Susana set their phone and tablet clocks back to the time they had arrived. Robby did the same with the bus radio.

The zombie dad walked to the warehouse

entrance. He waved at them.

Robby started the bus. He backed it out slowly.

Dante looked to his right. The ferrets jumped up and started rushing down the street toward them.

"Here they come!" Dante shouted.

The zombie dad began to run.

But his run was more of a slow, unsteady stagger.

They're going to catch him! Dante realized.

CHAPTER

BAIT FOR THE BEASTIES!

Doña Chabela's voice echoed in Dante's head: *Face your fears, boy!*

He had already stood up to one monster. Why not another half dozen?

Dante took a deep breath and clutched the fire extinguisher to his chest. Then he slammed his shoulder against the emergency exit lever at the back of the bus.

The alarm went off. His cousins started shouting at him to stop!

But Dante didn't listen. He jumped out of the bus and ran toward the zombie dad!

"Here!" he cried, shoving the extinguisher into Father's hands. "Protect yourself. I've got this."

He dashed off, looking over his shoulder. The ferrets looked angry—and hungry.

"Hey!" he yelled at them. "Y'all don't want him! Come get some fresh meat!"

Sniffing the air, the fire-breathing ferrets ran right past the zombie dad and continued hard on Dante's heels.

Dante felt heat on the back of his neck!

A couple hundred feet up the street, the big double doors of the zombies' warehouse swung open.

Almost there, Dante thought. *Just gotta stay ahead of the flames for another minute or two.*

Wait. How far can they spit their fire?

As panic hit, something strange caught Dante's eye.

On the side of the warehouse, someone had painted a message.

Protected by
Lord Micqui,
the Quiet Prince

"I'm trying to help the zombies, Your Royal Highness," Dante shouted. "If you can hear me, whoever you are, I could use some help!"

Only three more chapters to go! You can do it!

1 2 3 4 5 6 7 8 9 10 11 12 ○ ○ ○

CHAPTER

WHITE WEASELS!

Dante could feel the heat getting stronger. It was like standing too close to his dad's barbecue pit!

But the flames never touched him.

The zombie mom stepped through the open doors of the warehouse, waving him over. Dante pumped his arms and forced his legs to make one last push.

ZOOM!!!

He reached the warehouse and zipped inside. **BRRR!!!** It was super cold!

The zombie kids were waiting for him. He skidded to a stop, and they pulled him behind a towering shelving unit.

ROAR!!!

The ferrets came pounding into the building.

"Close up, Kalaan!" Mother shouted.

The doors slammed shut!

The fire-breathing ferrets turned this way and that, sniffing the air and growling.

Then they started calming down. They closed their mouths and sat on their haunches.

It was dark and very cold. Dante shivered. Big Brother put a blanket around his shoulders.

The giant weasels began to yawn. They lay down on the concrete floor, stretching lazily. Then something amazing happened.

Their gray fur started to change to snowy white!

"We did it!" Dante said, giving the zombie kids careful fist bumps.

Coming out from behind the barrier, he walked past the Furious Fire. They looked at him for a second, then closed their eyes and went to sleep.

"Thanks for everything," Dante told Mother, who opened the door a crack for him. Father slipped in, unharmed.

"No, thank *you*, dear friend," said Father.

"Have a safe journey home," Mother added, pulling Dante into a hug.

Their arms were cold, but Dante felt warm inside.

CHAPTER

14

PORTAL TO THE PAST

The bus was right outside, its door flung open.

"Hurry!" Robby called. "Something's up!"

Dante ran up the steps.

"That was pretty reckless," Ivan said. "But also super cool."

A hundred yards in front of the bus, a strange glow was filling the street. It expanded into a big circle. Through it, they could see the street in Nopalitos that had been blocked by a tree.

Except there was no tree now.

"What the heck?" Susana said.

Her brother shrugged and stepped on the gas, driving toward the portal.

Then they saw a woman dragging a tree into the street.

Doña Chabela! She ran off across someone's lawn.

"Whoa!" Dante gasped. "She made us take the detour!"

"What?" Malia said.

"It's the past," Ivan explained. "What time

did you set your clocks to?"

"I told them 7:55 a.m.," Robby said.

Ivan shook his head. "That's three minutes *before* we arrived!"

The portal began to close! The circle was getting smaller!

"Never mind! Go!" Malia shouted.

Robby stomped on the gas. The bus plunged through the portal!

CHAPTER

15

NOPALITOS, FOR NOW

The bus seemed to float on a stream of blue light. Dante could still see the street ahead. A bus pulled into view.

It was them! In the past!

After a few seconds, the bus turned onto the side street.

BLOOP!

It disappeared!

Dante felt the bus shake a little.

They were through the portal and back in Nopalitos. Dante, Ivan, and Malia hugged each other, cheering.

Then they noticed that Susana and Robby had gone limp. They were asleep!

The bus was headed right for the fallen tree!

"Robby!" shouted Malia. "Wake up!"

The bus driver shook his head and opened his eyes. "What? Oh no!"

He slammed on the brakes. The jolt woke Susana up.

Robby rubbed his face. "Looks like we have to take a quick detour."

He spun the steering wheel. The bus began to turn.

"No!" Dante shouted. "What are you doing?"

Robby entered the side street. The cousins held each other tight.

Nothing happened. The bus just bumped its way along the very normal road.

"What's wrong with you three?" Susana demanded.

"Susana, we just escaped," Dante reminded her. "Do you really want to go back to 13th Street?"

Susana blinked in confusion. "Thirteenth Street? Where's that?"

The cousins looked at each other. Ivan pulled the other two toward the back of the bus.

"They don't remember anything," he whispered.

Dante blinked. "Then how come we do?"

Malia put her hands on their shoulders. "Who knows and who cares? We're free!"

Dante looked out the window at the colorful houses of his town. "For now, at least."

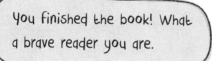

you finished the book! What a brave reader you are.

ACTIVITIES

THINK!

The cousins become friends with a family that is very different from them. Team up with one of your friends and make a list of the ways you are the same and different.

FEEL!

In the story, Dante is very afraid of fire, so the ferrets are his worst nightmare. Draw a picture of yourself standing up to the thing you're most afraid of.

ACT!

The ferrets are tamed by the cold. Here's a recipe for sweet icy treats:

1. Fill an ice tray with your favorite fruit juice or smoothie.

2. Cover it with plastic wrap.

3. Insert toothpicks into each square.

4. Pop the tray into the freezer.

5. Once it's frozen, enjoy your tasty ice pops!

DAVID BOWLES is the award-winning Mexican American author of many books for young readers. He's traveled all over Mexico studying creepy legends, exploring ancient ruins, and avoiding monsters (so far). He lives in Donna, Texas.

SHANE CLESTER has been a professional illustrator since 2005, working on comics, storyboards, and children's books. Shane lives in Florida with his wonderful wife and their two tots. When not illustrating, he can usually be found by the pool.